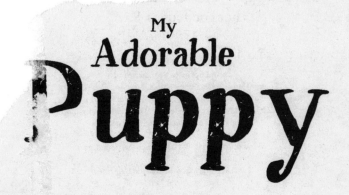

My
Adorable
Puppy

For Gavin Leonard, who is almost as much fun as a puppy, and for Auriol Bussell for all her good ideas. S.H.

Scholastic Children's Books
An imprint of Scholastic Ltd
Euston House, 24 Eversholt Street, London, NW1 1DB, UK
Registered office: Westfield Road, Southam, Warwickshire, CV47 0RA
SCHOLASTIC and associated logos are trademarks and/or
registered trademarks of Scholastic Inc.

First published in the UK by Scholastic Ltd, 2016

Text copyright © Scholastic Ltd, 2016

ISBN 978 1407 16216 4

Printed by CPI Group (UK) Ltd, Croydon, CR0 4YY
Papers used by Scholastic Children's Books are made
from wood grown in sustainable forests.

1 3 5 7 9 10 8 6 4 2

www.scholastic.co.uk

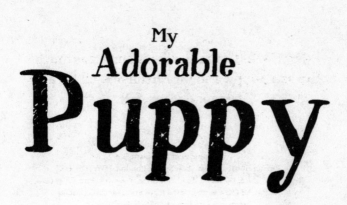

My
Adorable
Puppy

Sarah Hawkins

1

"Olivia! Where have you been?" Mum's voice made Olivia jump as she walked up to the front door.

Mum was unloading shopping from the car boot. "You should have been back ages ago! Dad and I were getting worried," she said, her face creased with crossness and concern.

"Sorry!" Olivia said. "I lost my bus pass so I had to walk home."

"Why didn't you just ask the bus driver for a ticket?" Mum said. "Didn't you have any money?"

"I did, but..." Olivia looked down at her feet. She hated talking to people she didn't know. Her face went all hot and her voice went funny. Mum knew that.

Mum sighed. Then she opened the door and lugged the shopping inside, telling Olivia off all the way. "You have to learn how to talk to people, darling. I can't believe Skye's so confident and you're so shy! No one would think you were sisters. And you have to be more responsible with your things. I can't believe you lost your bus pass again. And where's your school jumper?"

Olivia felt her tummy twist. She'd been hoping Mum wouldn't notice her missing jumper. "Upstairs?" she said hopefully.

"Olivia Jade Richards." Mum frowned at her over the shopping. "You would forget your head if it wasn't screwed on. Go up to your room until dinner's ready. You can tidy all your things and take care of them, for once. If I have to buy you *another* school jumper then it's coming out of your pocket money."

Olivia grabbed her school bag and ran upstairs. Her bedroom was on the very top floor, next to Dad's office, away from her parents' and Skye's rooms on the floor below. She shoved open the door and flung her rucksack on the floor. Her bedroom walls were lilacy purple and her bedspread was white with purple splodges, and it was hanging half off her bed. Her floor was completely covered with clothes and toys. Olivia took one look at it and flopped face-down on the bed. It wasn't her fault that she lost things. Things just sort of lost her... Even her pillow wasn't where it was meant to be.

And it wasn't her fault that she was shy. Not everyone could be like Skye. Her big sister could talk to anyone. While Olivia loved reading and animals, Skye loved singing and performing – she was in every school play. But even the thought of people looking at her made Olivia shudder. She couldn't think of anything worse! At least she and Skye looked alike, with their long sandy-blonde hair and blue eyes, otherwise Olivia might think that she was in the wrong family.

Olivia suddenly remembered the cosy spot she'd made the night before when she was reading her book. "Gotcha!" she said, grabbing her pillow from where she'd left it on the windowsill.

The spot at her window was one of Olivia's favourite places. Because her room was right at the top of the house, she could see over the neighbouring houses and right down to the sea.

Down on the beach a family were throwing a ball for a black-and-white border collie. A boy about Olivia's age threw a ball into the sea and the dog leapt in after it, barking happily. It swam, holding the ball proudly high above the water, then raced out and dropped it at the feet of its family.

Olivia knew what was going to happen next

and the family did too, but they weren't quick enough... Before they could move, the dog shook himself and water droplets showered all over them. Olivia giggled, and luckily so did the dog's family.

Olivia tucked her arms around herself as she looked at the happy dog. She'd wanted one for ages, but Mum and Dad always said she was too young. For a second, she thought about asking if she could have a dog for her birthday next month, but then she sighed. Mum would tell her that if she couldn't look after a school jumper than she definitely couldn't look after a puppy.

As the family left the beach Olivia turned and looked at her bedroom. Her jumper must be in here somewhere.

"Are you in trouble again?" Dad's voice came up the stairs.

"Don't come in!" Olivia cried. But it was too late. Dad pushed open her bedroom door and pulled a face. "This place looks like a bomb's hit it," he said, making a KABOOM noise. "A bomb made of plastic animals..." He moved a toy with his toe.

Olivia raced over and scooped it up. "Stop it, Dad! Anyway, you're untidy too. Your office is always a mess."

Dad laughed. "True! But I keep the rest of the house nice. Sometimes it's worth taking care of your things – when you have things that are worth taking care of, like you!" He pulled her into a hug. "Walk after dinner?" he asked.

Olivia nodded.

Dad always said how lucky they were to live by the seaside. He and Mum had lived in London when Skye was born, and they'd always dreamt of living by the sea. Luckily they'd moved when Olivia was little. She couldn't imagine living in the city.

Dad hated being indoors when he could

be outside at the beach. In summer he kite-surfed; in winter they went on long hikes, wearing so many layers they looked like marshmallow men, and had warm baths and hot chocolate when they got in. And they always walked after dinner when the weather was good. Sometimes Mum and Skye came too, but usually it was just Olivia and Dad.

"Come on then," Dad said. "I came up to tell you that dinner's ready." He picked up something from the floor next to her bed and threw it to her with a wink.

Her jumper!

🐾

The wind got stronger as they turned out of their road and on to the pathway that led to the beach. Olivia felt the wind buffeting her coat and whipping around her ears.

"Better than watching telly, eh?" Dad yelled into the wind. Olivia nodded. But somehow the beach wasn't making her feel as happy as it usually did. She couldn't stop thinking about the dog she'd seen earlier. She loved walking by the sea, but it would be so much better if she had a happy, fluffy little dog to share it with.

As Dad walked ahead, Olivia lagged behind. Then something caught her attention. A bit of paper was taped to a lamp post, but it was fluttering and flapping in the wind. Olivia went over to see what it was.

"RESPONSIBLE DOG-WALKER WANTED!" she read to herself, and her heart jumped. Below it was a picture of the most gorgeous puppy Olivia had ever seen! He was sitting and looking up at the camera with his mouth open in a doggy smile. He was small and cute, and he had golden fur and tiny triangular ears flopping down next to his big chocolate-brown eyes.

"Olivia!" Dad called.

"Coming!" she yelled back. The poster had given her a brilliant idea. Without letting Dad see, she tore it down and stuffed it in her pocket. Her heart was beating fast as she ran across the stony beach. Maybe if she could *prove* to Mum and Dad she was responsible, she might be able to get a puppy of her very own!

2

The next morning, Olivia sprang out of bed and raced downstairs. She wanted to talk to Mum and Dad before Mum left for work.

Mum looked surprised to see her. "What's going on?" she said. "I normally need to call up the stairs at least forty-seven times before you get up."

Olivia rolled her eyes, but then she stopped – she needed Mum and Dad to agree, quickly, before the people in the advert found someone else! She put the crumpled bit of paper on the table and smoothed it out. She'd been really careful not to lose it last night, even though it was so windy, and when she'd got home she'd put it safely on her pinboard, instead of leaving it in her pocket. It was one thing she didn't want to lose!

"Responsible dog-walker wanted," Mum read out loud. "I have an energetic three-month-old Labrador puppy, and I've broken my leg so I can't keep up! Dog-walker wanted for six weeks..." Mum trailed off and looked at Olivia.

Dad got up and started making himself some toast.

"Please can I do it, Mum?" Olivia said earnestly. "I can be responsible; I can. And it's not for ever. It's like a ... a trial run. And Dad and I go walking most nights anyway..."

Mum frowned. "I don't know, love. A dog is a huge responsibility. It's not all fun and games, you know. They need walking every day, not just when it's sunny. And you need to pick up their poo."

"I would!" Olivia said. Mum raised an

eyebrow. "I don't *want* to touch poo." Olivia felt a bit sick at the thought, but then she remembered the tiny puppy's grinning face. "But it would be worth it," she said firmly.

"I'm sorry, darling..." Mum shook her head.

"Dad?" Olivia asked desperately.

"I don't know, sweetheart. If you lose someone else's dog..." Dad shrugged.

"I WON'T," Olivia burst out. She'd been so sure that Mum and Dad would say yes. It wasn't like she was asking for her own dog this time. She could feel hot tears building behind her eyes and she crossly wiped them away. "You say I can't have a dog until I'm responsible, but you won't let me *try* and be responsible!"

"Olivia..." Mum started, but Olivia couldn't hold back the tears any more. She ran out of the kitchen, stomping all the way up the stairs to her room.

In her bedroom Olivia grabbed her pillow and ran to the windowsill. As she went she trod on a bit of Lego and a sharp pain spiked though her foot. She gave a howl and started to cry properly, burying her head in her pillow. Outside the rain pelted down on the window, like the whole world was crying with her. *It wasn't fair!*

There was a soft knock on the door.

Mum and Dad stood in the doorway, Dad's arm around Mum's shoulders. Mum held out the crumped bit of paper. "OK," she said with a smile, "we'll give it a go."

🐾

Olivia felt a wobble of nerves as she ran the doorbell. "Coming!" a voice called, and a second later the door swung open. The lady had a pink cast from her knee all down to her foot. Her bare toes were sticking out the end and her toenails were painted sparkly pink too.

Olivia felt her voice disappear and she hung back behind Mum as the lady invited them in. Dad squeezed her shoulder reassuringly.

"It's such bad timing," the lady said, walking stiffly though the house. "My husband's away and I just can't keep up with Barley like this!"

Barley. Olivia hugged the name to her. She'd been so excited last night that it had been hard to go to sleep. It had felt like Christmas Eve! Mum had phoned the number on the poster and Mrs Blythe had been delighted that they wanted to help out. Her house was only a few streets away, and she'd invited them all around to meet her dog the next day.

"I'll fetch Barley and you can meet him," Mrs Blythe said.

She opened the kitchen door and a yellow furry puppy bounded towards them, grinning so widely that his little pink tongue was hanging out. "Awwwww!" Mum and Skye said together. Olivia couldn't even speak. He was the most gorgeous thing she'd ever seen.

While Mum and Skye chatted to Mrs Blythe, Olivia knelt down and Barley galloped up to her, putting his front paws on her knees and licking at her ear. Olivia giggled and stroked his head and down his back. His golden fur was so soft and fluffy; his belly was chubby and round, and his paws were surprisingly heavy on her leg.

"Barley's twelve weeks old," Mrs Blythe said. Barley whipped around at the sound of his name and his wagging tail bashed Olivia's arm. Olivia giggled again and Barley turned around and nuzzled into her as if he was saying sorry.

Skye came over to stroke him too.

"He needs two fifteen-minute walks a day," Mrs Blythe said, "and a lot of playing with. He's a bit more of a handful than I realized. I work at home, you see, and my husband thought that it would be good for me to have some company. And then I tripped over his dog bowl and..." She tapped the cast on her broken leg. "I can barely get around, let alone take an energetic puppy out. My husband is working abroad and can't get back for six more weeks. I'm so grateful someone wanted to walk him."

"Well, it's really Olivia who's going to be your dog-walker," Mum told Mrs Blythe. "Someone will be with her, of course, but she's the one who wants to do this. Say hello, Olivia."

Olivia could feel her face going hot as she looked up from where she was stroking Barley. "Hello," she said in a half whisper.

"She's a bit shy," Mum explained, "But she loves dogs. She's hoping that she can prove she's responsible enough to have one of her own."

Mrs Blythe looked at Olivia and Olivia held

her breath. "OK," she said with a nod. "Well, Barley certainly seems to like you, and as long as you're willing to deal with the poop?"

Olivia nodded. Barley had been lying quietly on her lap, but now he sat up too as if he was waiting for his owner's decision.

"What do you think, Barley?" Mrs Blythe asked.

Barley stared up at Olivia seriously. Then he gave her a big lick on the chin.

Mrs Blythe grinned. "I think that's a yes! OK, kid, you're hired."

"Yes!" Olivia jumped up, and Barley leapt around too, barking happily.

As Mum, Dad and Mrs Blythe had a cup of tea, Olivia and Skye played with Barley. He went and got a chewy toy and showed it to Olivia, then raced off with it when she tried to take it. Olivia couldn't help laughing at the energetic little pup. He was so adorable!

Mrs Blythe gave them a spare key so that

Olivia could come in before and after school and take Barley for his walk. "All the things you'll need are here," she said, showing Olivia where the leads, doggy treats and poo bags were in the garage. "Don't let him off the lead, and watch that he doesn't pick anything up in his mouth while he's out," Mrs Blythe told her, staring at the puppy scampering around their feet. "He chews anything he can get his paws on."

Olivia nodded, trying to take it all in.

"He really seems to like you," Mrs Blythe said with a smile. Olivia bent her head shyly, her hair covering her face, but she felt a warm glow inside.

"Would you be able to take him out today?" Mrs Blythe asked.

"Can I?" Olivia turned to Mum and Dad excitedly.

"OK," Mum said. "Skye and I have to go to the shops, but you and Dad can go."

"Over to you, Olivia," Mrs Blythe said.

Olivia's tummy felt full of nerves and excitement as she led Barley back into the garage. She was going to take a real puppy out for a walk! Barley followed her excitedly, and when he saw her reach for his lead he jumped up, put his front paws on her legs and grabbed it. "Good boy!" Olivia stroked his soft ears. He wasn't just cute, he was clever too! Remembering what Mrs Blythe had said about him chewing things, she took the lead out of his mouth and put it on the side while she filled her pockets with poo bags and doggy treats.

"Ready?" Dad called.

What else had Mrs Blythe said she needed? Feeling like she'd forgotten something, Olivia led Barley out of the garage. Dad and Mrs Blythe were standing by the front door.

"Let's go!" Dad said cheerfully.

Olivia nodded, but she still felt like

something was wrong... Suddenly she realized – she'd forgotten to pick up Barley's lead! *Oh no,* Olivia thought. She couldn't forget something so important before she took Barley out for the very first time! "Um, I just need to..." she muttered, but when she turned to go back to the garage, she saw Barley had something in his mouth. The lead! He must have picked it up when she'd forgotten it!

"Good boy, Barley!" Olivia said, taking the lead and clipping it on to his collar. "You and me are a team already!"

"Woof!" Barley barked as if he was agreeing. Then he pulled Olivia towards the door.

"OK!" Olivia laughed. "Walkies!"

3

Olivia felt so proud as she walked Barley out on to the seafront. None of the people they passed would know that she was just looking after Barley; they'd think he was really hers!

He tugged on the lead with surprising strength, and Olivia found herself running a bit to keep up. Dad laughed. "Don't let him run away with you," he said, bending down to pull on Barley's lead. The little dog looked back at him curiously.

"Keep a firm hand and show him who's boss," Dad said.

Olivia looked at Barley's cute little face.

She couldn't imagine telling him off or bossing him around. He was just too adorable!

"Sit!" Dad said to Barley in a firm voice.

Barley cocked his head to one side and wagged his tail.

Olivia giggled.

"It's important that dogs are trained," Dad said. "What if he runs out towards a road and you can't get him to stop? It's like having a little kid."

"You always used to make me wait for the green man to cross the road," Olivia said.

"Exactly," Dad replied. "It's to keep you safe. And Barley will be safer if he can obey commands. Barley, *sit!*"

Barley looked up at them with his chocolate-brown eyes, and Olivia felt her heart melting. "He's only little!" she said, bending down to give him a hug. She couldn't stop stroking his soft fur. When she rubbed him behind his floppy triangular ears his cute stumpy tail wagged happily.

"He'll learn! We'll have to look online about how to train a puppy," Dad said cheerfully. "It's all part of being a good dog owner."

Olivia smiled. Dad was talking about Barley as if he'd be theirs for ever!

"I used to have a dog when I was growing up – did you know that?" Dad said as they walked along. "He was called Bruce and he was a cocker spaniel. He was such a smart dog. Once he got out of the house and came to school to pick me up!"

They walked all along the pier. Barley trotted in a zigzag, going from one interesting smell to another. Every person they met with a dog said hello to Olivia. The first time she just smiled back shyly. The second time it was a lady who had a big dog with curly fur. He went to sniff hello to Barley and made the little puppy jump. He skittered behind Olivia's legs.

"It's OK, Barley," Olivia reassured him. "Don't be frightened."

"He's a gorgeous puppy. How old is he?" the lady asked.

Olivia looked at Dad appealingly. He knew she hated talking to strangers.

Dad rolled his eyes at her. "He's three months old," he told the lady.

As she and Dad talked, Barley crept out from behind Olivia's legs and bravely sniffed the dog. As soon as he did both their tails started wagging happily, and soon they were rolling around together.

Once they'd untangled their leads and walked off, Dad nudged Olivia. "Barley is braver than you!" he said.

"Why?!" Olivia exclaimed.

"He wasn't too shy to say hello!" Dad laughed.

Dad spoke to lots of different people as they went along. Everyone exclaimed what a gorgeous puppy Barley was, and every time they did Olivia felt a swell of pride.

As they turned a corner, Barley went over to a patch of grass. "Uh-oh," Dad said.

"What?" Olivia watched as Barley sniffed the grass then turned in a circle and squatted down. "Oh no! Gross!"

Dad shrugged. "It's got to be done. Every gorgeous little puppy is full of stinky poo!"

Olivia felt sick as Dad showed her how to put a plastic bag inside-out on her hand. "The bag is between you and the poo, so you're not really touching it," he explained.

Olivia stepped forward. She had to do this if she was ever going to prove she was responsible enough for a dog of her own. She hated people that left rubbish on the beach. She closed her eyes, put the bag over her hand and picked it up.

"Gross, gross, gross, gross!" she shrieked, but she had done it. Dad took the bag and tied it up neatly. "Well done, sweetheart," he grinned. "No one likes picking up poop, but it's important, especially on the beach or in parks where children play. Come on, I'll get you an ice cream."

"I don't think I want one," Olivia said queasily.

Barley ran over to her and jumped up, putting his paws on her knees. She ruffled his ears and stroked his golden fur. "OK, I suppose it is worth it to have you," she said, leaning over to put a kiss on his soft head.

They walked to the café at the end of the pier. Olivia and Barley sat down on the stony beach while Dad went and got Olivia's favourite ice cream – swirled vanilla with strawberry sauce.

"What's he got in his mouth?" Dad asked as he walked back. Olivia jumped up and looked at Barley. While she wasn't looking he'd picked up an old plastic bottle from somewhere and was chewing on it.

"Oh no!" Olivia cried, fishing it out mouth. "Don't eat that, Barley."

"You have to watch him," Dad said, "And if he goes quiet, that normally means he's doing something naughty."

Dad gave her the ice cream and they sat watching the waves, Barley lying next to them. Olivia felt a bubble of happiness as she stroked Barley and licked her ice cream. Looking after the puppy was even better than she'd imagined it would be.

As she grinned down at him, Barley suddenly scrambled on to her lap, his little puppy tail wagging back and forth. It took Olivia a second to realize what was happening, but then he lunged at her hand. Barley wanted to eat her ice cream!

"Help! Dad, help!" Olivia shrieked as she tried to hold the ice cream out of the reach of the excited puppy. She held it up in the air as Barley climbed on top of her, woofing happily.

"Down, boy! Sit!" Olivia giggled. But it was no good; Barley wouldn't listen. Soon she was covered with ice cream and the naughty puppy was licking it off the pavement. And Olivia had never been happier!

4

As the bell went, Olivia's tummy jumped nervously. She normally loved English, but they were doing Project Talks, where each person had to write a presentation and then say it out loud in front of the rest of the class. Olivia had chosen to do her presentation on dogs, and she'd loved learning more about them – but she was dreading having to read it out loud.

Over the last few weeks Olivia had been walking Barley twice a day. She and Mum and Skye had walked him that morning, and Olivia had told Mum and Skye that she was worried about her talk.

"Why don't you practise on us?" Mum had suggested as they'd walked along. "Here," she sat down on a bench. Skye sat next to her and Barley sat in-between their feet. Two pairs of blue eyes and one pair of chocolate-brown ones looked at her expectantly.

Olivia had groaned.

"Come on, it'll be good practice," Mum had said.

"My project is on dogs," Olivia started.

"Woof!" Barley had barked delightedly.

Olivia had giggled. "People have had dogs as pets for thousands of years. There are 400 million dogs in the world, and there are hundreds of different types. Labradors are the most popular pet . . . that's you, Barley." Olivia broke off to stroke Barley's ears.

"Go on, you're doing really well," Mum had said encouragingly.

"Dogs can smell 1,000 times better than humans. Dogs are omnivores like us, which means they eat meat and vegetables in their dog food. Some human food, like chocolate, is poisonous to them."

Mum nodded.

"In Ancient China the emperors often kept tiny Pekinese dogs up their sleeves. The first living being in space was a dog called Laika. And there's more but I can't remember the rest," Olivia finished in a rush.

"It sounds like you know lots of things," Mum had said. "I didn't know that bit about Pekinese dogs. You couldn't fit Barley in anyone's sleeve!"

"I liked doing the project – I just wish I didn't have to say it all out loud in front of everyone," Olivia had grumbled, going to sit on the bench. Barley had whined sympathetically.

"You just need to pretend they're not there," Skye had told her.

Olivia couldn't imagine her confident big

sister ever getting nervous. "But you *like* being on stage," she said.

"Yes, but I still get worried before I have to go on," Skye told her. "Even famous actors do."

Olivia was about to reply, but she had to run to stop Barley from chewing a plastic bag that he'd found under the bench.

"Puppies grow out of chewing things at around a year old," Olivia had told Mum and Skye, once they'd taken it away from him.

"See, you're going to be fine," Mum had said.

As she sat in the classroom, Olivia didn't feel fine. Her friend Emily had done a speech about her favourite band and Maya had done one about art, but Olivia couldn't concentrate as her friends talked. She just kept wondering when it would be her time to stand up. Her tummy was swirling and churning like there was a hurricane blowing inside it. How did everyone else find it so easy when she found it so difficult?

"Right, next to speak is Olivia," Ms Crouch, her teacher, called.

Olivia walked up to the front of the class. Her face already felt hot and embarrassed, even though she hadn't said a single word yet. As everyone turned to look at her, Olivia felt her face go even redder. She couldn't speak. She shook her head and rushed back to her seat.

"OK, never mind. Next time, Olivia," Ms Crouch said kindly. Olivia nodded, feeling like she was going to cry. Emily reached over and squeezed her hand.

Olivia put her head on her arms. It had gone awfully, just like she knew it would. If only she wasn't so shy!

🐾

Olivia rang the doorbell twice, then opened the door with Mrs Blythe's keys. "Hi, Barley!" she laughed as Barley galloped towards her like a furry cannonball.

"Woof, woof!" he barked, as if he was telling her all about his day. Olivia felt all her upset about the talk fall away as she saw his little face. She sat down so she could fuss him all over, and Barley wriggled delightedly, his tail wagging so hard it bumped against the floor.

Mrs Blythe limped in. "I'm so glad you're here. He's been pestering me all day!"

Barley put his head on one side and gave Olivia an innocent look, as if he was saying that he'd been good. Olivia gave him a reassuring stroke behind his ears and he wagged his tail happily.

"Do you think you could give him a long walk tonight?" Mrs Blythe said. "I've got a hospital appointment and I don't want him here on his own, getting into mischief."

Olivia nodded, secretly feeling delighted. More time with Barley!

"Is that a yes?" Mrs Blythe said, her

eyes twinkling.

"Yes, please," Olivia said shyly.

"Fabulous," Mrs Blythe replied. "And be careful with him chewing things. He tried to eat one of my shoes this morning. Luckily I only need one at the moment!" She wriggled the toes coming out of her plaster cast.

Olivia giggled, but Barley nudged her with his head and whined.

"OK," she laughed. "Walkies!"

Barley scrambled to his feet so fast that he almost toppled over. "Rruff!" he barked excitedly.

Olivia followed him into the garage and picked up all the stuff they needed. But when she went to clip his lead onto his collar, Barley had a red chew toy in his mouth.

"You can't take that out with us," Olivia told him. But when she tried to take it away, Barley wouldn't let go! He pulled it like he and Olivia were in a tug of war. He was in a naughty mood!

"Oh, please, Olivia, be an angel and take him out!" Mrs Blythe called. "I need some peace and quiet around here!"

Olivia looked at Barley and pulled a face. "Come on, before we get in trouble!" she whispered. "We can run around and bark as much as we like outside!"

Dad was waiting for them at the end of Mrs Blythe's drive, holding a big basket.

"What's that?" Olivia asked.

"Wait and see," Dad said mysteriously.

Barley was so pleased to be outside that he jumped around excitedly, tangling his lead around Olivia's legs as he rushed to sniff the doorstep, then raced to sniff the basket. "Oof! Help!" Olivia laughed. "He's in a troublesome mood," she explained as Dad helped untangle her.

"Don't worry, a nice walk will sort that out," Dad said. "I thought we could go all the way to the secret beach. It should be quiet enough there to let him off his lead."

Olivia grinned. Mum and Dad called it the secret beach because hardly anyone knew about it. All the tourists went to the big beaches, so the secret beach only ever had a few people on it. It always felt like it was just for them.

"You're going to love it, Barley!" she reached down to give him a hug. "And Mrs Blythe asked me to take him out for a long walk."

"Perfect!" Dad said.

They headed on to the seafront, then turned on to the coastal path that wove over the hills.

At the top of the hill they stopped and had a drink of water, giving Barley some to drink in a bowl that Dad had thought to put in the basket.

Barley lapped at the water happily, his little bum sticking up in the air. The sun had come out and it was now a beautiful day. Olivia and Dad looked out over the sea. Down below they could see the cove, with its crescent-moon-shaped sandy beach. The clifftop curved around, with a long spit going out to sea, ending in a crumbling archway. The sea glinted and shimmered invitingly in the sunshine.

Suddenly, Olivia couldn't wait to be down there. "Let's go. Last one there has to pick up Barley's poo!" she laughed, running downhill as fast as she could, Barley racing along next to her, matching her stride for stride. His tail streamed out and his fur ruffled in the wind as he ran.

Apart from a few families walking and making sandcastles, the beach was completely deserted. Olivia stroked Barley all over. He dropped down and rolled in the sand, panting happily.

"Now will you tell me what else is in the basket?" Olivia asked.

Dad grinned. "This is my puppy training kit!" He unpacked all the things he'd brought. There were doggy treats, chew toys, a frisbee and a library book called *How to Train Your Puppy*.

"Are we going to teach him to read?" Olivia joked.

"The book's for you, cheeky," Dad said. "I spoke to Mrs Blythe and she'd love us to start training Barley. He's at the perfect age – he won't even know he's learning; he'll just think it's fun!"

Barley went over to investigate, and grabbed a doggy treat out of the basket.

"Hey, come back with that, you naughty pup!" Dad laughed.

Barley settled down to start chewing it.

"Good thing I brought spares!" Dad smiled. "Right, do you want to try taking him off the lead?"

Olivia glanced down at Barley, who had

finished his treat and was sniffing around the basket interestedly. She couldn't help feeling nervous. What if they lost him? He was so little. "I don't know," she said anxiously.

"Puppies aren't good at coming when there are other distractions around," Dad explained. "So you can only take them off the lead in quiet places. But when they're very little like Barley, they want to stay close to us because we make them feel safe."

Olivia stroked Barley.

"Mrs Blythe says that they've done this with him before, so don't worry," Dad said. "Just let go of the lead rather than taking it off, and then it'll be easier to catch him if we need to."

Nervously, Olivia let go of the lead. It trailed in the sand behind Barley as he trotted around the basket.

"Now let's have a little walk," Dad said.

He picked up the basket and they

wandered slowly down the beach. Olivia kept looking back at Barley. What would he do? Would he run off and get lost? Barley turned around in surprise as they went without him. He leapt up and raced after them, barking, "Woof, woof!"

"He's saying, 'Wait for me!'" Olivia laughed.

"Brilliant. Now we make a big fuss of him and give him a treat for coming to us," Dad said. "Good boy! Well done, Barley!" He reached down to ruffle Barley's ears.

Olivia gave him a treat and he gobbled it up. "Clever boy!" she told him.

They wandered slowly around the beach with Barley trotting happily at their side. When he went to sniff a rock pool, Dad changed direction and Olivia followed. After a second, Barley looked up in alarm, then galloped towards them, his ears flapping in the wind.

"Good boy!" They praised him again and

gave him more treats.

"That's enough for today," Dad said. "Let's see if we can get him to sit."

But before Olivia could grab the lead, there was a shout from along the beach.

"Sorry!" a boy yelled as a tennis ball flew towards them, heading for the sea.

"Uh oh!" Dad said.

"Barley, stay!" Olivia called, but it was too late. The little puppy bounded delightedly after the ball. "Stop that puppy!" Olivia shouted.

5

Olivia raced over as Barley splashed into the sea. He looked surprised, and barked at the waves. Then he galloped in and doggy-paddled up to where the tennis ball was floating.

"He's fine!" Dad said.

Barley jumped through the waves and back to Olivia, barking delightedly. He dropped the ball at her feet and started to roll in the damp sand, covering his golden coat with brown streaks.

"You mucky pup!" Olivia laughed, picking up the lead and holding it tightly. She was just pleased that he was OK.

"We can't take him back to Mrs Blythe like this!" Dad said.

Barley looked up at Olivia proudly, his tongue hanging out. Olivia realized what he was going to do about a second before he did it. She started to move, but she wasn't fast enough. Barley shook himself and covered her with mucky, sandy water!

"Argh!" Dad cried out as Barley splattered water all over them. "There's only one thing for it," he said, wiping the mud off his legs. "We're going to have to go swimming!"

"But we don't have our costumes!" Olivia replied.

"I'll phone your mum," Dad said. "She and Skye can bring them and we can have an evening at the beach. How does that sound? It should still be warm for an hour or two."

Olivia agreed, and when Dad phoned home, Mum and Skye did too.

Dad, Olivia and Barley walked around the

beach, keeping Barley safely on the lead this time, until Mum arrived in the car.

"Any excuse to get in the water!" Mum grinned as she unpacked Dad's surfboard.

"Thanks, babe," Dad grinned, giving her a kiss on the cheek.

"I brought snorkels for us!" Skye told Olivia.

Mum and Skye already had their costumes on, but Mum held a towel around Olivia so she could get changed.

Once she was ready, Olivia paddled into the sea. It was a bit chilly, but she knew it would warm up when she started swimming around.

She went into the waves and called for Barley. There was no one left on the beach now, so Dad took him off his lead again. He splashed after her, wagging his tail, then splashed out again, running excitedly across the beach to Mum.

While Dad kite-surfed, Skye and Olivia snorkelled. It was so sweet to be able to look underwater and see Barley's tiny puppy legs paddling beneath the surface. Skye and Olivia played catch, and Barley swam between them, trying to get to the ball. Finally, Olivia passed the ball to him, and he grabbed it and paddled out of the water, taking it up on to the beach. Then he flopped down and started chewing it.

"Hey! Give us our ball back!" Skye laughed. "I guess that game's over!"

As Olivia followed Barley out of the water, the sun went behind the clouds. Mum noticed Olivia shivering and looked at her watch. "Right, time to be going home, I think. Mrs Blythe will be wondering if we've kidnapped Barley."

Mum wrapped Olivia in a towel, and used the edge of it to wipe Barley's fur. But even though he shook himself, his coat was still sticky and stiff with sand and seawater.

"I think he needs a proper wash," Mum said with a sigh. "This is not what I expected to be doing tonight, but how do you feel about bathing a puppy?"

"Hear that, Barley?" Olivia wrapped her towel around Barley and gave him a soggy hug. "It's bath time!"

❧

Dad and Skye decided to walk home while Mum and Olivia took Barley back in the car. Mum wrapped Olivia and Barley in towels and they sat together on the back seat. Olivia kept hold of Barley, but he didn't wriggle at all; instead he gave a puppy yawn and curled up on her lap.

Olivia couldn't stop grinning. It had been such a fun afternoon and, best of all, she didn't have to give Barley back just yet.

She snuggled up to his little warm body, and closed her eyes for a second...

When Mum woke her up, they were back home. Olivia yawned in surprise, and Barley sat up and yawned too. Then he started wagging his tail again, already full of energy.

Mum showed Olivia a photo on her phone of her and Barley sleeping. "You two are so cute!" she smiled. "Right. Let's get you cleaned up. I'd better take Barley; I don't want him wandering off in the house. It's not puppy-proof, and goodness knows what he'd find to chew!"

Olivia felt so excited as Mum carried Barley inside and up the stairs. Somehow having him in the house made him feel more like hers than ever.

Olivia's hair felt sandy and she wished she could hop straight in the bath, but she knew she had to look after Barley first. She followed Mum as she carried the little pup into the bathroom.

"Shut the door properly – we don't want a damp puppy escapee!" Mum said.

As Mum started running the bath. Barley

stood up on his back paws and peered over the edge.

"He likes it!" Olivia grinned. "Shall I put the bubbles in?"

"No, I don't think that bath bubbles are good for dogs. You have to use special doggy shampoo to wash them, but we don't have any, so we'll just use nice warm water," Mum said. "It should get the worst of it out, anyway."

Mum lifted Barley in, and the two of them started pouring warm water over his messy fur.

"Good boy, Barley," Olivia soothed him.

Mum tested that the water wasn't too hot, then started using the shower hose to rinse him. Barley looked at it curiously, then started drinking from the spray.

They rubbed Barley's fur like they were shampooing their hair, being careful not to get any water in his ears. His wagging tail splashed them, but neither of them minded. Barley was just so cute!

Barley's fur looked completely different when it was all wet. It looked much darker than usual. There was a muddy patch on his face, so Olivia gently rubbed it with a flannel, then spiked up the fur on the top of his head. "Look, Mum, he's got a Mohican!" she laughed. She tried to flatten it down with the flannel, but Barley grabbed it and started chewing on it.

"OK, let's get him out," Mum said. She lifted him onto the bath mat, and they covered him with a towel then started rubbing his fur dry. Barley tried to wander off, but Olivia held him firmly. "Who's a good boy!" she praised him, and his wet tail started wagging under the towel.

When they took off the towel Barley's fur was back to its usual golden colour and it was already looking much fluffier and softer. He was just as gorgeous as before.

"Right," Mum said, "I'm going to take

this naughty one home. You get in the bath. Where are your shoes?"

"Um…" Olivia's tummy gave a guilty jump. The last time she'd seen them was on beach when she'd got changed…

"Olivia!" Mum scolded.

"I haven't lost anything for ages!" Olivia cried. "And besides, I was busy being responsible for Barley." She thought about when he ran off the lead. "At least I didn't lose him!"

"Hmmm," Mum said. "I guess we should be grateful for that." Barley had started chewing the bath mat. "Your shoes are probably floating out to sea right now. You'll have to ask Dad nicely if he'll go and look for them tomorrow. Barley!" Mum told him off and took the bath mat out of reach. "Right, mister, you're going home."

"Bye, Barley," Olivia said, kissing him on his soft, clean head. She wanted to take Barley back to Mrs Blythe's, but she was cold and her hair was stiff with saltwater. Suddenly a warm bath sounded really nice.

Mum started the bath for Olivia – one with bubbles this time – then she led Barley away.

As Olivia got into the warm water she thought about what a fun afternoon it had been. It was hard to believe that it was the same day as her disastrous talk. Barley had made her forget all about it!

After a while she got out, and put on her favourite puppy pyjamas and her fluffy slippers. She was on her way downstairs when she heard a noise. It sounded like a bark – but it couldn't be ... could it?

6

Olivia raced down the stairs in her pyjamas. The lounge door was shut, but as Olivia went up to it she heard the bark again. She opened the door and Barley jumped out, wagging his tail happily.

Olivia couldn't believe it. "What are you still doing here?" she laughed as she bent down to stroke the wriggling puppy all over.

Mum turned around on the sofa and sighed. "Mrs Blythe asked if we could keep him overnight – she's had her cast taken off her leg today and she's in a lot of pain. What could I say? Dad's gone to pick up his basket and all the things we'll need. Barley's been sat by the door waiting for you!"

Barley flopped on to his back and waved his legs in the air, asking for a tummy rub. Olivia giggled happily. This was better than she could have ever imagined! Then she thought of something that would be even *more* wonderful...

"Can he sleep in my room?" she asked breathlessly.

"No!" Mum said firmly. "He's going to sleep in the kitchen. That way if there are any puppy accidents, they'll be easy to clean up."

"Oh," Olivia protested, but she didn't really mind. It would have been amazing to have Barley in her room, but it was still brilliant to have him stay overnight. A sleepover with her favourite pup – what could be better!

🐾

After dinner, Dad suggested they watch a film. They all went into the lounge, with Barley trotting next to Olivia. All evening she had been racing around trying to stop Barley running round the house and chewing things. If she turned her back on him for a second he was getting into trouble!

"I thought we'd have worn him out with our busy afternoon!" Olivia said after she had to jump up from her dinner for the third time and stop him from chewing a box of tissues.

"Puppies are full of energy!" Mum had told her. "But you're doing brilliantly. If he was ours we'd have to keep the house extra tidy so that there weren't things lying around for him to get his paws on."

Olivia nodded thoughtfully.

Mum set the film up, then she and Dad flopped on one sofa. Skye and Olivia took their usual place on the other sofa, but Barley trotted around not knowing where to go. "Come on, Barley." Olivia patted the seat next to her. Barley did a big jump and landed on her lap! She stroked his velvety ears and he flopped down, his head resting on her knee like a pillow, his bum next to Skye.

"How come I get the stinky end!" Skye protested, but Olivia knew she didn't mind really. They both petted the warm puppy as he snuggled up between them.

Barley gave a huge yawn. Olivia grinned. He was even cuter when he was sleepy!

The sisters stroked him as he snoozed. In the middle of the film Olivia heard a funny noise and looked around. Mum and Dad caught her eye, and Mum giggled and pointed to the little pup. Olivia looked down as he let out another noise. Barley was snoring!

Instead of watching the film, Olivia couldn't tear her eyes away from the snoozing puppy. She traced her fingers over his velvety ears, down his back to his stubby tail. She even looked at his little paws, with their tough black pads and neat little claws. As she stroked, Barley's legs started to twitch and his mouth started moving.

"He's having a dream!" Skye said.

"Even when he's asleep he's chewing things!" Olivia whispered.

Olivia looked around in delight. She felt tired out from the day and clean from the bath. Mum, Dad and Skye were all grinning and Barley was sleeping on her lap. She felt a warm feeling inside. It felt *right* that Barley was here.

🐾

"OK, bedtime," Dad said when the film finished. "All little girls and little dogs need to be asleep."

He came over and picked up the sleepy puppy. Barley opened his eyes and his tail wagged gently as Dad took him into the kitchen. Olivia followed. Dad put Barley in his basket, but he jumped straight out again.

Olivia laid out his water and food bowls next to the basket in case he got hungry in the night. Barley sniffed all around them and nibbled on a few crunchy bits. Then he looked up at Olivia as if he was saying, "What next?"

"Bedtime, Barley," Olivia told him. She patted the basket and Barley jumped inside, lying down happily.

Olivia gave him one last stroke. "Night, sleep tight," she whispered. But as she tiptoed to the door, Barley bounded out of the basket and tried to follow her!

"No, Barley!" she laughed. "You have to stay here. Basket," she said firmly.

Barley whined but he got into his basket and rested his head on his paws sleepily. Olivia patted his head and his tail wagged.

"Goodnight, Barley. I love you," she whispered as she left the kitchen and closed the door.

"Sleep well, love." Dad kissed her on the

top of her head. Olivia went and hugged Mum and Skye goodnight, then went upstairs to her room.

As she lay in bed, she thought about Barley sleeping in his basket downstairs. She loved him so much. She never thought having a dog would be so much work – or so much fun.

Olivia suddenly realized something terrible. She sat up in bed and clicked her light on, feeling as bad as she had when she had to give her speech. She'd started walking Barley to prove that she was responsible enough for a dog of her own. But now she didn't want just any dog – she wanted Barley!

7

When she woke up, Olivia ran down the stairs two at a time. She couldn't wait to see Barley.

Dad was coming out of his room, ruffling his hair sleepily.

"Morning!" Olivia tore past him and went into the kitchen.

Barley was sitting on the other side of the kitchen door when she pushed it open. He jumped up at her excitedly, his tail wagging. Then he tore away from her, his feet slipping in his haste to get to the back door. He jumped up at it, whining urgently.

"I think he needs a wee," Dad said as he

padded into the kitchen and poured a glass of water.

Olivia quickly clipped on Barley's lead, then opened the door so he could go out and do his business in the back garden. Barley almost pulled her over as he cantered down the steps.

He sniffed around for a bit, then went into a flower bed and cocked his leg. Olivia glanced inside. "It's a good thing Mum didn't see you weeing on her rose bush!" she giggled.

Barley rushed around like a tiny golden whirlwind, jumping up at Olivia's legs, then racing off to sniff the rest of the garden. Finally he came over and sniffed Olivia's furry slippers.

Olivia bent down to stroke him and he jumped up at her delightedly, licking every bit of her he could reach.

"I'm happy to see you too," Olivia told him. "What shall we do today?" Yesterday had been so much fun, and today was Saturday. She could spend all day with her favourite puppy!

"I'm afraid we have to take Barley home straight after his morning walk," Mum said from the back door.

Olivia's happy plans vanished.

"Sorry, darling," Mum said, "but he has to go back to his real owner. We're only looking after him, remember?"

Olivia thought back to her realization from last night and felt gloomy all over again. Once Mrs Blythe's leg was better, she wouldn't be walking Barley any more.

"How long does it take to walk normally after a broken leg?" she asked, following Mum back inside.

Mum poured some puppy food out for Barley and he raced over to his bowl and started chomping it up. "You've got another two weeks of looking after Barley, so make the most of it," Mum said. "But he has to go home today. Besides, you have nice plans with your friends this afternoon, don't you?"

"Yes," Olivia replied sulkily. Emily had invited her and Maya around to her house. Olivia knew it would be fun, but she didn't want to leave Barley. If she only had two weeks left she wanted to spend every minute with him. And she didn't want him to go home. It just felt so right that he was here in her house. She wished he could stay for ever.

She tickled his ears in the way he loved and he flopped over on his side so that she could stroke his silky-soft tummy. "I love you, Barley," she told him.

Barley looked at her seriously, his head on one side. Then he raced over to his bed, and came back with his favourite red chew toy. He dropped it at her feet and wagged his tail happily. "Thanks!" Olivia giggled. "Does that mean you love me too?"

She hugged Barley as he chewed happily

on the toy. "Oh, Barley," she mumbled into his soft fur. "What am I going to do without you?"

"I think you should dognap him," Emily said. "You could tell Mrs Blythe he got lost, and then just keep him."

Olivia shook her head. "I can't do that!" she laughed.

Emily, Olivia and Maya were sprawled on the grass in Emily's back garden, making daisy chains. Olivia had hated taking Barley home after his walk that morning, but she'd felt better as soon as she saw her friends.

They'd had a fun afternoon bouncing on Emily's trampoline. Emily did gymnastics and could do all kind of cool flips and twists. Maya and Olivia had tried to copy her, but had ended up lying on the trampoline, giggling as Emily had bounced them around. Once they'd finished, Olivia had told her friends all about the naughty puppy and how she'd realized she loved him. Emily and Maya were trying to think of things that would help, but Olivia knew it was no good.

"I know, we could buy him from her!" Maya suggested.

Olivia shook her head again. "I don't have any money. Besides, she wouldn't just sell him."

"Sounds like she's a rubbish owner anyway," Emily said.

"She's not," Olivia sighed. It would be easier if Mrs Blythe was a horrible person, like a baddie in a Disney film, then she could take Barley away and everyone would cheer. But it wasn't like that. Olivia loved Barley, but she knew Mrs Blythe loved him too. Once her leg was better and Mr Blythe was home, they'd go back to being a family.

Emily's scruffy dog, Biscuit, snuffled over and Emily put the daisy chain on his furry head like a crown, then hugged him around the neck. "I couldn't imagine not being able to keep Biscuit."

Maya had a hamster, and she nodded too.

Olivia petted Biscuit's shaggy fur and he rolled onto his back. Olivia giggled. Biscuit was a little terrier and he looked completely different to Barley, but they both liked a good tummy rub!

"At least you have your birthday party to look forward to!" Emily said.

Olivia nodded. With everything going on with Barley she'd almost forgotten about her birthday, but now it was only a week away.

"What are you going to do for your party?" Maya asked, twirling her short black hair.

"I don't know," Olivia said, biting her lip. Skye had had a big party this year and invited her entire class, and Mum had said Olivia could do the same, but the thought made

Olivia's tummy feel wriggly and nervous.

"You should go to Splash World – the water slides are so much fun," Emily suggested.

"Or ask if you can do pottery painting," Maya said. Maya loved making things. Her crafts always looked so good – but Olivia's somehow always turned out rubbish.

Olivia laughed. "I'm not very good at art. The thing I like most is being with Barley…" She stroked Biscuit absent-mindedly as she thought about her party. What was she going to do?

"Emily!" her mum called from inside. "The girls are going to have to go home soon so that we can go and visit Auntie Meg."

"Oh, Mum!" Emily pulled a face. "I don't want them to go yet."

"Well, they won't want to come with us!" her mum replied.

"Maybe you could come and help me take Barley for his walk tonight?"

Olivia suggested shyly.

"YAY!" Emily cheered. "Can we, please?"

Emily's mum shrugged. "If it's OK with both your mums, it's OK with me. You'd better phone and check."

Olivia ran to the phone. Luckily her mum said yes and Maya's mum agreed too. Olivia couldn't wait! She was so excited about showing Barley to her friends. They were going to love him!

That evening Olivia met Emily and Maya outside Mrs Blythe's house. "I'll just go in and get his things," said Olivia. "Back in a second."

There was a woof and a patter of feet inside the house, then Barley jumped up at the front door. They could see his little golden shape and his tiny paws pressing up against the glass.

"Oh, he's so cute," Emily whispered.

"You don't have to whisper," Olivia laughed.

She opened the door and shooed Barley inside. He jumped up at her legs excitedly and she bent down to ruffle his ears. She quickly gathered everything she needed and clipped his lead on to his collar.

"I'm taking Barley out, Mrs Blythe," Olivia called.

"OK," she yelled back, "Have fun!"

The little puppy galloped at her heels as they went down the pathway. Emily and Maya squealed and bent down to pet him. Olivia felt proud as she showed Barley off.

"He is the sweetest thing I've ever seen!" Maya said.

"He's so much smaller than my dog," Emily added.

"He'll grow," Mum said. "He's still only a puppy."

"Labradors get much bigger than terriers like Biscuit," Olivia told her.

As Olivia walked along she chatted with her friends, but she also kept an eye on what Barley was up to. She made him sit before they crossed a road, and rewarded him with a treat when he sat down on his plump bottom. When he did his business she scooped it up without any fuss.

"Bleugh, I couldn't do that," Maya said squeamishly.

"I didn't think I could, either," Olivia confided to her. "But you get used to it. And it's worth it to hang out with my favourite ball of fluff!"

She knelt down and Barley jumped up to lick her chin.

"You're really good at looking after him," Emily said.

Olivia felt her cheeks go hot, but for once she wasn't embarrassed, she was happy.

When they got to a quiet bit of beach, they let Barley off his lead and threw a ball for him.

All three girls loved seeing him scampering along. Barley loved going to fetch the ball, but he wasn't very good at getting it back. They had to chase him and stop him from chewing it!

"This is so much fun," Emily laughed as Olivia managed to get the ball back from the excited puppy for the third time.

"I wish Barley could come to your birthday," Emily said.

"Well, he could if you had a picnic party," Mum suggested. "We could have it on the beach."

"That's a brilliant idea!" cried Olivia. "Can I, Mum?"

"If that's what you want," Mum said.

Olivia looked at the excited puppy scampering around. "Yes, please," she grinned. If Barley can come, it'll be the perfect party!

8

"Happy birthday to you! Happy birthday to you!"

Olivia opened her eyes sleepily as Mum, Dad and Skye burst into her room. Mum was carrying a cake that was shimmering with candles.

"Quick, before we set off the smoke alarm!" Dad sang as Mum sat on the end of the bed and held out the cake. "Happy birthday to you!"

"Oh, wow," Olivia giggled as she sat up in bed. The cake was shaped like a puppy asleep in a doggy basket! Nine candles twinkled in the basket base.

"Make a wish," Mum said.

Olivia shut her eyes. *I wish,* she thought as hard as she could, *I wish Barley could be mine, for ever.*

Then she blew as hard as she could, and her family cheered as all the flames disappeared at once.

"And I think *I* got a wish come true too," Mum said, looking around Olivia's bedroom. "It's so tidy in here! What happened?"

Olivia shrugged. She didn't want to tell Mum, but secretly she hoped Barley might be able to stay in her room if he slept over at their house again. The thought of the little puppy curled on the end of her bed had been enough to make her tidy everything up. She knew it wasn't very likely that Mum would let him, but it was worth it, just in case.

"Never mind all that – open your presents!" Dad said, dumping some brightly wrapped parcels on her lap.

Olivia grinned as she tore into the paper.

But when she opened the first package, her heart sank. It was a bright red dog bowl. "Thank you!" she said, hoping she sounded enthusiastic. She knew what the next one was just from feeling it. She ripped open the paper, and a purple lead with stars on it fell out.

"Open mine!" Skye said, giving her a present wrapped in yellow spotty paper. Inside was a plastic scoop with a bag attached to the back.

"It's so you don't have to touch the poo any more," her big sister laughed, making a face.

With each parcel, Olivia felt even worse. *What was the point of having doggy things if she couldn't have Barley?* "Thank you," she said, trying to sound excited.

"Don't you see what it means?" Mum said, snuggling next to Olivia in bed and putting her arm around her. "These aren't your main present, silly. These are things you'll need *for* your present. You're getting a dog for your birthday!"

"As soon as we stop looking after Barley, we'll go to the rescue centre and find a dog who needs a home," Dad said. "We're very proud of the way you've looked after Barley. You've proved that you're responsible enough for a dog of your very own."

Olivia looked at her family's excited faces and felt worse than ever. Whatever dog they got, it just wouldn't be Barley! As she started to cry she hid behind her long blonde hair, but her tears rolled down her nose and plopped on to her birthday cake.

"What's wrong?" Mum cried. "This is what you've wanted for ever!"

Olivia sobbed as Mum squeezed her tight.

"Come on, let's get breakfast started," Dad said to Skye. They picked up the cake and headed downstairs.

"Now what's all this about?" Mum asked,

turning to wipe Olivia's tears off her face and kiss her on the top of the head. "Hmmm? These don't seem like happy tears to me."

Olivia sniffled. "It's Barley," she managed to sob. "I love him. And I wish he was mine."

"Ah," Mum said softly. "But, darling, you knew he had an owner right from the start."

"I know," Olivia said sadly. "But I love him so much. And he loves me, Mum, I know he does."

"I know he does too, darling. It's clear to everyone how much that puppy adores you," Mum said kindly. "But he doesn't belong to us. He already has a family. And there are a lot of dogs out there that need a loving home. Won't it be lovely to be able to pick any dog you want?"

Olivia nodded.

"Right then, no more tears. You need to get ready for your party!" Mum said brightly.

"OK," Olivia replied. She gave Mum a

smile, but inside she still felt like crying. No matter what anyone said, it was no good. The only dog she wanted was the one she couldn't have.

❧

Olivia got dressed in the special party dress Mum had bought her. It was as blue as the sky on a sunny day, and as velvety and soft as one of Barley's ears.

When she was dressed she finally started feeling excited about her birthday party. Her friends were meeting down at the beach, except for one – the most important guest of all!

Barley's tail started wagging as soon as he saw her and he gave an excited bark. Olivia bent down so she could stroke him and he leapt all over her delightedly.

"It's my birthday, Barley," Olivia told him. Barley looked up at her, his mouth open in a doggy grin. "And you're invited to my party. Would you like to come?" Barley tilted his head to one side as if he was thinking about it. Then he gave a happy bark and jumped up to lick her face.

"I think that's a yes!" Olivia said with a laugh.

"We're going down to the beach to have a birthday picnic," Mum explained to Mrs Blythe.

"Have fun! And happy birthday," Mrs Blythe said. "Barley and I got a little something for you, but…" She pulled a half-chewed present out from behind her back.

"Barley!" Olivia said with a laugh.

"He loves chewing the wrapping paper!" Mrs Blythe exclaimed. "Anyway, I hope you like it."

Olivia opened the present. Inside were some socks with puppies on. "They're lovely, thank you!" she said, giving Mrs Blythe a hug.

"No, thank *you*. I don't know how Barley and I would have coped without you. He really loves you," Mrs Blythe said.

"I love him too," Olivia said, laughing as the naughty pup jumped at her legs, trying to get the crumpled-up wrapping paper. Olivia threw it for him and he chased after it, his tail wagging happily.

"Come on, let's get to your party. It can't start without you," Mum said.

❦

Olivia walked along the seafront with Barley.

"We're just round ... here!" Mum said as they turned a corner on to a grassy field beside the beach.

Olivia gasped as she caught sight of balloons and bunting. Emily was there – and she'd brought Biscuit along too! There were tables laid out with a birthday feast, and blankets for everyone to sit on. Maya and Skye held up a banner with HAPPY BIRTHDAY and a drawing of Barley on it. Granny and Grandpa Avery were even there, even though they lived far away!

"Surprise!" Granny said, bending down to give Olivia a massive hug. "And this handsome chap must be Barley!"

Olivia said hi to everyone, and they all admired Barley. Then Dad gathered them together for a group photo. "Say 'Barley'!" he cried.

"Woof!" Barley replied, making everyone laugh.

Mum showed Olivia all the presents stacked up under the table.

"What do you want first, presents or games?" she asked.

"Presents!" Olivia cried.

She sat in the middle of a picnic rug opening presents and exclaiming over the gifts. Barley had so much fun playing with the wrapping paper, running through it, and – of course – chewing it. Mum was on Barley babysitting duty so that Olivia could have fun with her friends without worrying about the little pup.

"Shut your eyes and hold out your hands," Granny said. Olivia did and Granny put a little present into her palm. It was wrapped in pretty blue-and-yellow paper. She ripped it open and there was a puppy-shaped chocolate inside.

"Yum, thanks!" Olivia grinned, throwing her arms around Granny.

"It's just a little something," Granny said. "You'll see your big present when you come and stay with us next. It's a trampoline!" she said in a whisper.

Grandpa gave her a squeeze. "Granny's already had a bounce on it," he said, a twinkle in his eye.

"Time for games!" Mum said. "Who's up for

hide-and-seek?"

Olivia and her friends played a breathless game of hide-and-seek, with Grandpa bellowing like a giant as he tried to find them. "Fi-fie-fo-furl ... I think I've found the birthday girl!" he roared, peering over a bush where Olivia was hiding. Olivia squealed.

Finally Grandpa had found everyone, and they all ran laughing back over to the blankets. Olivia flung herself on the picnic rug next to Barley, exhausted but happy.

"That was so much fun!" Emily giggled.

Olivia stroked Barley's head, then noticed he had something in his paws. "What are you chewing *now*?" she laughed. But as she bent down to take it away from the naughty puppy, her body turned cold and she gasped out loud. A horrible feeling ran all the way through her. "Mum!" she yelled out, holding up the chewed blue-and-yellow paper.

Mum was holding Barley's lead as she talked to Emily's parents. She looked down in surprise when Olivia shouted.

"Mum," Olivia gasped, trying to hold back panicky sobs. "Mum! Barley's eaten chocolate – and it's poisonous to dogs!"

9

"OK, don't panic," Mum said, sounding a bit panicky. She bent down and looked at Barley, who grinned back at her happily. "He seems OK, but let's take him to the vet just to be on the safe side. Are you sure he ate it?"

Olivia nodded. The tears were coming fast now, hot and wet as they trickled down her cheeks.

"Stay at your party. I'll take him," Mum said.

"No!" Olivia protested. "I'm responsible for him. I'm coming too."

Mum looked at her and nodded. Then she grabbed her car keys. "Lara, can you tell the others where we've gone?" she asked Emily's mum.

"Of course," she agreed. "And don't worry, I'm sure he'll be OK. Biscuit once ate a whole pack of Lego and he was absolutely fine."

Barley ran alongside Mum and Olivia as they rushed to the car. His tail was wagging like they were having a great adventure. He didn't seem poorly, but Olivia felt ill. Mum opened the car and she climbed in the back, holding Barley next to her, the way they had when they came back from the beach. They'd been so happy then.

When the car started moving, Barley whined and put his head on Olivia's lap.

"Mum, hurry!" Olivia cried.

"It's OK, it's OK," Mum said. "He's probably just feeling a bit sick." But she drove extra fast through town.

Olivia stroked Barley's ears all the way there. "I love you so much, Barley," she sobbed into his fur. "You're such a good boy." His tail wagged gently.

When they got to the vet, Mum screeched the car to a halt and flung the door open. "Take him in while I park," she cried.

Olivia jumped out of the car and Barley trailed after her. He was moving slowly now and he didn't look like his usual happy self at all.

The door of the vets' jangled as Olivia and Barley went inside. Waiting on plastic seats were a man with a cat in a cat box, a lady with a little dog who sat up interestedly as Barley came in, and a girl about Olivia's age with a rabbit on her lap.

As everyone looked at her, Olivia felt her voice fade away. Her face went hot and she could feel her heart beating fast. But she had to do something – Barley needed her!

"Please," Olivia gasped. "Please help. My dog's eaten chocolate."

All at once lots of things happened. The lady behind the reception called for a vet, and took Barley away. Then Mum burst in and Olivia burst into tears.

❧

Olivia sat in the waiting room in her special birthday dress. Mum had her arm around her, and everyone was being really nice. The receptionist had given her a hug and a drink of water. The girl had let her stroke the rabbit and the lady with the dog had told her a story about when her dog had disappeared when they were out for a walk. "My silly boy chased a squirrel," she told everyone, "and then got lost. It was four hours before we found him." She squeezed the little dog and he panted happily. "I was so worried, but he was absolutely fine. And I'm sure your puppy will be too."

Olivia gave a shaky smile.

Finally, the vet walked in. Mum stood up and Olivia grasped her hand tightly. *Please let him be OK. Please, please please,* she thought desperately.

"He's OK," the vet smiled.

Mum sighed in relief and Olivia started to cry again. "It's all right!" Mum said.

"I know, I'm so happy!" Olivia sniffed.

"We've given him some medicine and he's been a bit sick, but he'll be absolutely fine," the vet explained. "It was very responsible, rushing him here like that. He's lucky to have such a good owner."

"Oh," Olivia said. "I'm not his owner, I just look after him."

"Well, then, he's lucky to have such a good friend," the receptionist said kindly.

"We'll keep him in overnight, but he'll be as right as rain tomorrow," the vet said. "And just as naughty as before!"

Mum and Olivia skipped back to the car.

But before they got in, Mum stopped and her face creased with worry.

"What?" Olivia asked.

"It's OK," Mum said. "I just realized something. We're going to have to tell Mrs Blythe…"

❖

It was late at night, but Olivia wasn't in bed. Instead she was sat at her desk, writing down a very important speech. Tomorrow was her last day of walking Barley, and she had to do something.

After Barley's chocolate-chewing accident, Olivia and Mum had gone back to the party and told everyone that Barley was going to be fine. Luckily Mrs Blythe had been really nice when Mum had called her. She'd said that Barley chewed anything if you took your eyes off him for a second, and that it was just an accident. She had even said thank you to

Olivia for reacting so quickly – without her, Barley could have been really poorly. Olivia could tell it like a funny story now, even though she remembered how scary it had been at the time.

They'd played lots more games and had a really fun afternoon, then once Olivia's friends had gone home they'd had fish and chips on the beach with Granny and Grandpa. It had been a good birthday after all – and something Granny had said had given Olivia an idea.

"That puppy is such a handful, they must need a lot of help with him," she'd said.

That was why Olivia was still awake. She chewed the end of her pencil thoughtfully. Mrs and Mrs Blythe were so busy, maybe even now Mrs Blythe's leg was better they might need some help.

Olivia picked up her speech and went to stand in front of the mirror. She looked at her reflection and took a deep breath.

"Dear Mrs Blythe," she practised saying. "Barley is so energetic, he needs lots of walks and playing with, and he'll need even more as he gets older. Maybe I can keep walking him? I could walk him once a week so you and Mr Blythe could have a night off. I love Barley and I would love to help out..."

Olivia put the paper down with a sigh. It was OK saying it to herself, but how would she ever say it to Mrs Blythe? She thought about her speech at school, her face turning red and her voice disappearing. But then she thought about talking at the vet's. When it mattered, she'd been able to talk in front of strangers. Olivia looked at her reflection determinedly. She had to do it – or she'd never see Barley again.

❖

The next day, Olivia stood nervously in Mrs Blythe's lounge. Mrs Blythe was walking around normally now, and was even wearing a pair of high pink heels. Olivia stroked Barley's soft fur as he came up to greet her. "Wish me luck, Barley," she whispered.

"Are you taking him straight out?" Mrs Blythe asked.

"Um, yes, but I wanted to talk to you first," Olivia said, her voice sounding a bit squeaky.

"Oh?" Mrs Blythe raised an eyebrow. "Go on then, I'm all ears!"

Olivia brought out her paper and took a deep breath. "Dear Mrs Blythe, Barley is so energetic—" she said in a rush.

"He certainly is," Mrs Blythe laughed. Then her phone rang. "I'm so sorry, darling, I've got to answer it – it's Mr Blythe," she said. "I'll be right back."

"Hello!" she said, walking into the next room and swinging the door behind her. It wasn't completely shut and Olivia could see her pacing up and down as she talked.

She felt a tugging at her feet and looked down. Barley was chewing on one of her shoelaces.

"Barley!" she said. "Haven't you learnt your lesson about eating things?"

Barley looked up at her curiously. "Woof!" he said.

Olivia bent down to stroke him. She hoped Mrs Blythe would say yes. She'd miss seeing Barley every day, but even if she could just walk him once a week that would be OK. After all, a little bit of Barley was better than nothing.

"I know that!" Mrs Blythe's voice rose crossly as she talked into the phone. "But what else can we do? You can't turn down this job."

Olivia's heart jumped. She knew she shouldn't be listening but she couldn't help it. Maybe Mrs Blythe was going to be away for longer and Mrs Blythe would need more help with Barley!

"Well, if the job's in Australia, that's where we'll have to go," Mrs Blythe said firmly. "We're just going to have to move."

Olivia gasped out loud. Mrs and Mrs Blythe were taking Barley to Australia!

"Sorry about that," Mrs Blythe said, coming back into the room. "Now, you wanted to ask me something?"

Olivia put her speech behind her back and shook her head. If Barley was going to be on the other side of the world, there was no way she could walk him. She felt all her hope leak out of her like air from a burst balloon.

Mrs Blythe was still looking at her and Olivia was sure her face was going red. "Um, where are the dog treats?" she mumbled.

"Here!" Mrs Blythe gave her a new packet of doggy treats. "Enjoy your walk!"

"We will," Olivia whispered. She managed to take Barley outside before the tears came. She sank down onto the doorstep and buried her face in Barley's soft coat. He whined softly and she stroked him. "It's OK, Barley," she sniffled. "You'll like Australia. There are lots of beaches to run around on there."

Barley buried his nose in her neck, then reached up and licked a tear off her cheek.

"Oh, Barley, I'm going to miss you so much!" Olivia sobbed.

10

Olivia was up in her bedroom, looking miserably out of the window at the beach far below. Downstairs, she heard the doorbell ring, and then her parents' murmuring voices, but she didn't go down to see who it was. She was looking at the photo of her and Barley asleep in the car, and the one of everyone from her birthday party, before Barley had chewed on the chocolate.

As Olivia got up to put the photos on her pinboard, she heard a funny scratchy, scampery noise on the stairs, and then her door burst open. There was Barley, looking clean and golden and silky soft, and with a big blue bow around his neck.

"What are *you* doing here?" Olivia gasped, bending him down to give him a hug. Barley flopped over onto his back, holding one leg in the air for a tummy rub.

"Your room had better be tidy!" Mum called as she, Dad, Skye and Mrs Blythe all piled inside. "Goodness knows what he might eat!"

"It's tidy!" Olivia said, looking at everyone in confusion. What was going on?

"Can I sit down?" Mrs Blythe asked. "My leg's still a bit sore."

Olivia nodded, and Mrs Blythe perched on the end of her bed. She sighed, and sat forward. "I've got something to ask you, Olivia," she said seriously.

Olivia nodded again. Maybe Mrs Blythe was going to tell her about moving to Australia. She bit her lip and tried not to cry. Barley settled down on her lap and she ran her fingers though his soft fur as she waited to hear the bad news.

Mrs Blythe took a deep breath. "Would you have Barley?" she asked.

Olivia didn't understand. "Have him?" she asked.

"Would you have him for good? Would you adopt him?" Mrs Blythe gave a little smile, but Olivia felt like her face was frozen. She looked at Mum, Dad and Skye. Mum and Dad were grinning, and Skye did a little skip on the spot.

"She looks so surprised!" Skye said, taking a photo.

Olivia glanced at Mum and she nodded encouragingly, looking like she was about to cry.

"Adopt him?" Olivia echoed. "So he'd be mine?"

"For ever," Mrs Blythe said. But then she couldn't say anything else because Olivia was hugging her as if she'd never let go.

Barley jumped up and down, and suddenly he leapt on the bed too, barking excitedly.

"Mind Mrs Blythe's leg!" Mum called.

"It's OK!" Mrs Blythe laughed. "Is that a yes, then?"

"Yes! YES!" Olivia shouted.

"Woof, WOOF!" Barley joined in.

"You're going to be mine!" Olivia said, hugging Barley. He scampered on to her lap, jumping up and licking her chin and every bit of her he could reach.

Salty tears were pouring down Olivia's cheeks as she buried her face in Barley's soft fur. She still couldn't take it all in.

When things had calmed down, they all went downstairs for a cup of tea. As they sat at the kitchen table, with Barley lying at their feet, Mrs Blythe explained.

"We have to move away, and we can't take Barley with us. We're only going to have a tiny apartment, and it just wouldn't be fair on an energetic dog like him. I love him but I didn't really know how much work he'd be. Maybe

I should have had to prove I was responsible before I got him..." She reached over to put her arm around Olivia's shoulders. "But it's all turned out OK, because I think he was meant to be with you."

Olivia stared down at the puppy – her puppy – in delight. She still couldn't believe it. Barley gazed up at her, his tongue hanging out in a puppy grin, looking as heart-meltingly cute as he had when she first saw his picture on the poster. She now knew that he was a lot more than cute. He was naughty, he was energetic, he needed lots of love and care – and he was hers. The bow on his collar had swung down under his chin like a bowtie, and he scratched at with his foot, then looked around the kitchen as if he was searching for something to chew. He wasn't perfect, but he was absolutely perfect for her.

❖

"Welcome home, Barley!"

Olivia jumped up and down on the front doorstep. It had been three days since her birthday wish had come true, and today was the day that Barley was finally moving in for good.

Mr and Mrs Blythe arrived with Barley trotting in behind them. Mr Blythe was a tall man with a moustache and a kindly smile. Olivia liked him straight away.

Mrs Blythe bent down to give Barley a goodbye stroke. "Be a good boy," she said, wiping a tear from her eye, "and don't chew too much of Olivia's stuff."

"And no chocolate!" Mr Blythe added.

Mrs Blythe came over to give Olivia a hug. "You've got our address and my email address too. Make sure you send me lots of updates about how Barley's doing."

"I will," promised Olivia.

Mrs Blythe handed her the lead, and Mum

and Dad walked them to the door. Barley stepped after them, but Olivia held his lead tight.

"You're staying here," she told him. "You live here now, with me."

She bent down to give him a hug and Barley's tail started wagging happily. Olivia felt a burst of happiness. Barley was really hers.

"Let me show you all your things, Barley," she said.

She led him into the kitchen. His food and water bowls were laid out on a plastic mat near the back door, which had a new dog-flap in it. Barley ran over and sniffed them, then started lapping at the water with his little pink tongue. "Look, the bowls have your name on them," Olivia showed him. She and Emily had made them at a pottery-painting place, with lots of help from artistic Maya. They both had BARLEY written on them in bright colours.

The water bowl had paw prints all around it, and the food bowl had bones on it.

"And your basket is right…" Olivia trailed off as she looked around the kitchen. Barley's basket wasn't where she'd put it last night.

Mum, Dad and Skye came in from waving Mr and Mrs Blythe goodbye.

"Where's Barley's basket?" Olivia asked.

"Ah, well," Mum smiled, a mischievous look in her eye. "Dad and I decided that we'd put it somewhere tidier…"

Olivia looked around the room. Then Dad pointed to the ceiling, a broad smile on his face.

"My room?" Olivia squealed.

Her parents nodded.

"But only if he doesn't keep you awake," Mum said.

"He won't!" Olivia rushed over to give her parents a hug. Barley jumped up at their legs, woofing happily.

"Come on!" Olivia ran up both flights of stairs. Barley scampered ahead, then paused to make sure she was following him.

Olivia burst into her room. There, under the window, was Barley's dog basket.

Mum, Dad and Skye appeared in the doorway and watched as Barley sniffed around the basket, and then climbed inside.

"It's perfect!" Skye grinned.

Olivia agreed. Now Barley was there, home was perfect.

🐾

Olivia walked up to the front of the class and turned to face everyone. Emily gave her a thumbs-up.

"My Project Talk is on Australia," Olivia started. She could feel her face going hot, but she kept talking anyway. "My penpal lives there. She sends me lots of postcards and emails and tells me all about life over there."

She held up a postcards of a gorgeous beach filled with surfers, and another of a kangaroo in front of a massive red rock.

As Olivia continued with her talk, she started to feel more confident. She was speaking and the whole class was listening happily. Best of all, she knew she had a surprise at the end that everyone was going to love.

"Even though it's nearly Christmas here, it's summertime in Australia, so it's really hot there. They are going to have Christmas Day on the beach, and eat a barbecue instead of Christmas dinner!" Olivia pulled a face and the class laughed.

"When I write back, I tell my penpal all about my dog, Barley." Olivia held up pictures of Barley that Mum had printed off for her. "Mrs Blythe used to own Barley before I adopted him. He's been mine for three months now, and he's grown a LOT."

She showed everyone the photo of Barley at her birthday party, and then showed a more recent one of Barley on the beach, holding a stick in his mouth. He was almost double the size. Olivia found it hard to believe that he'd ever been so tiny.

"What type of dog is he?" Paul asked.

"He's a Labrador," Olivia told him with a grin. She didn't feel shy at all when she was talking about Barley. "In fact..." She looked at her teacher, who nodded. Olivia opened the classroom door, and Skye came in, holding a lead. Barley trotted behind her, wearing a Santa hat! He came and sat down proudly next to Olivia. He wasn't the chubby puppy he used to be; he was now a long, lean young dog. He almost came up to Olivia's middle as he sat next to her, his tongue hanging out in a doggy grin. He looked like an enormous version of the cute puppy on the poster Mrs Blythe had put up all those months ago.

The entire class started talking at once, then they crowded around Olivia and Barley. Barley sat happily as they all stroked him.

"That was a *very* good talk, Olivia," Ms Crouch said kindly. "There are only five minutes left of class, so why don't you and Skye take Barley out before he eats the classroom..."

Olivia looked over and saw that Barley had someone's pencil case in his mouth. "Barley! Barley!" Olivia called. "Give that back!"

Olivia and Skye took Barley out into the playground. Mum and Dad were standing there, wrapped up in winter hats and coats. They were talking to Emily's mum, who was waiting there with Biscuit. Barley raced over to sniff hello to his doggy best friend.

"How did it go?" Mum asked.

"Brilliantly!" Olivia replied, "I was hardly nervous at all. And everyone loved Barley!"

"Of course they did!" Mum grinned. "Well done, darling, I'm so proud of you."

Barley and Biscuit were sniffing each other happily. Barley was much bigger than the little terrier now, but he didn't seem to realize his size. He thought he was still the tiny puppy he'd been when he and Olivia had met.

As the dogs started chasing each other around the playground, playing in the autumn leaves, Dad gave Olivia some gloves. "We thought we could go for a quick walk to the secret beach," he suggested. "It might be cold, but our dog still needs his walk!"

"I know!" Olivia grinned. "I'm a very responsible dog owner."

"Yes, you are," Mum agreed, kissing her on the top of her head.

Olivia watched Barley racing around and grinned. Her puppy was just as energetic as ever. He still loved walks, swimming and chewing everything he could get his paws on. Mum was hoping he'd grow out of it, but he hadn't yet.

Olivia still loved walking him, and best of all, now when their walks were over, he came home with them, watched TV on the sofa with the rest of the family, and then slept on the end of her bed like a furry hot-water bottle. Olivia couldn't believe how lucky she was.

"Then tomorrow we're going Christmas shopping," Mum continued. "We have to get ready for Barley's first Christmas – and I know just what to buy him."

"What?" Olivia asked, checking Barley wasn't listening.

"A whole roll of wrapping paper he can chew!" Mum laughed.

Olivia giggled. "Barley!" she called. He came galloping over, nearly knocking her off her feet. "Sit," she said, and he plonked himself down. She reached down to clip his lead on to his collar. He was so well trained now that he didn't really need it, but they still kept him on the lead near busy roads to keep him safe.

"Where's your scarf?" Mum asked Olivia as they waved goodbye to Emily and Biscuit and walked out of the playground.

"Um..." Olivia had been hoping her parents wouldn't ask about that.

"Let me guess – did Barley chew it or did you lose it?" Dad asked.

Olivia shrugged apologetically. "A bit of both... First he chewed it, and then I left it on a park bench..."

"You two are as bad as each other!" Mum exclaimed. "Well, at least we know one Christmas present you'll be getting!"

"Sorry, Mum!" Olivia hugged her around her middle.

Barley gave a soft whine, as if he was saying sorry too.

"OK!" Mum laughed. "Let's go!"

As Mum, Dad and Skye walked off ahead,

Olivia bent down to give Barley a hug. She still couldn't believe that she had got to keep him for ever.

"I love you," she said, kissing his soft head.

"Rruf!" Barley replied.

Olivia laughed. She gave him one more hug, then stood up. "Wait for us!" she called. Then she and Barley ran after the rest of their family.

Puppy
Care Tips!

Are you a responsible dog owner like Olivia? Read our Puppy Care Tips to learn about looking after your very own adorable pet!

Bath Time!

Olivia has to give Barley a bath after the naughty pup has an unexpected swim. Here are our top tips on bathing your puppy:

You will need:

- 🐾 A helpful adult
- 🐾 A doggy brush
- 🐾 Tasty treats
- 🐾 Doggy shampoo
- 🐾 A towel
- 🐾 And a dirty pup!

1. First, brush your dog with a doggy brush to get all the tangles out of his coat. Remember to be very gentle – no one likes having their hair pulled!

2. Some dogs can be very nervous about having a bath. If it's your dog's first bath, put him in the empty bath and give him a treat before you bathe him, just to show him that baths aren't scary.

3. Run a shallow bath of lukewarm water – not too hot and not too cold

4. Ask your helpful adult to put your dog in the water. If your dog is still nervous, give him another treat.

5. Using the shower hose or a cup, wet his fur from the neck down. Avoid the eyes, ears and mouth.

6. Once your dog's fur is wet, rub in some doggy shampoo until he's nice and bubbly.

7. Rinse all the bubbles away using the hose or cup.

8. If your dog's head is dirty, carefully wash him with a flannel or a damp cloth, but don't get any water in his ears, eyes or mouth.

9. Lift him out of the bath and rub him with a towel. Most pet stores sell super-absorbent pet towels. Your dog will want to shake or rub himself on the furniture to get rid of the water, so be careful or you might get wet too!

10. Have an after-bath party! It's important to show your dog that bath time happens before fun time! Why not play his favourite game or give him his favourite dinner along with lots of love and attention. He'll be so soft and silky that you won't be able to resist cuddling him!

Staying Healthy!

Naughty Barley chews everything and had to go to the vet because he ate some chocolate. Do you know about the foods that dogs are allergic to?

Here are some foods that your dog shouldn't eat:

- Avocado
- Alcohol
- Caffeine (tea and coffee)
- Chocolate
- Onions and garlic
- Grapes and raisins
- Macadamia nuts

If your dog eats any of these then you should take him to the vet.

At the Vets!

All animals need to go to the vet to make sure they stay happy and healthy. But sometimes going to the vet can make animals nervous. Here are our top tips for keeping your puppy relaxed:

1. Take your puppy for a walk first. This means he'll be calmer, and it also means he's less likely to have an accident!

2. In the waiting room, give your dog lots of strokes and cuddles.

3. Take his favourite treats or his favourite toy with you to make him feel at home.

4. If your dog has a favourite basket or blanket, you could take that too.

5. Talk calmly to him in a happy voice. This will help him realize that there's nothing to be frightened of.

6. When the visit is over, make sure you reward your puppy with lots of love and attention. After all, he's been very brave!

Olivia isn't the only one with an adorable pet
– read on for a sneak peek of the next adorable
adventure:

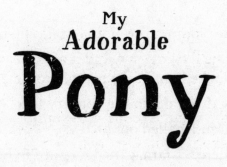

My
Adorable
Pony

Clara looked out of the car window excitedly as they drove down the country lane. "We're here!" Mum called out.

"Where?" Clara leaned forward in her seat and peered outside. "Where are we?" Mum and Dad had been so mysterious about their day trip. They wouldn't tell her where they were going, but just said that they were taking her for a surprise. Clara was desperate to find out what it was!

As Dad slowed down, they drove past a big sign. "Hollyhock Stables," Clara read out loud, then gasped. Stables meant one thing – ponies! Clara loved ponies. She had always been horse-mad ever since she could remember. She loved the way they looked, their long, beautiful manes and their kind eyes. She'd read lots of books about unicorns, but to Clara, horses and ponies seemed just as magical. But what were they doing at a stable? "Are we going to see some horses?" she asked. Then she had a brilliant thought and squealed in excitement. "Am I going to have a riding lesson? That would be AMAZING!"

"Hold your horses!" Dad joked as he parked the car.

Mum turned around in the front seat. "You know how you've asked for a pony for every birthday and Christmas present since you were little?" she said with a grin.

Clara nodded, twirling her finger in her long brown hair.

"Well, Daddy and I got a bit of extra money recently," Mum said. "And we thought we could have a nice holiday, or a new car . . . or we could spend it giving you what you want most in the world."

"You're getting a pony!" Dad said, with a massive grin. "Or a horse. Whichever one is smaller."

"A pony," Clara told him automatically. Then she realized what he'd said. "I'm getting a pony?" she squealed. She glanced from Mum to Dad and they both nodded. Clara didn't know what to say. This surprise was better than she could ever have imagined! "Thank you! Thank you SO MUCH!" she shrieked.

Mum opened the car door and Clara burst out to hug her. Then she ran round the other side to give Dad a squeeze too.

Mum laughed. "Come on, a lady's waiting to show us some ponies!"

With Mum and Dad following behind, Clara skipped through the gate and up to a big yard surrounded by stalls and, beyond them, fields. In one field, she could see a big, patchy black-and-white horse and a smaller grey pony. They were galloping around, their manes streaming out behind them. Clara stopped to watch. She was grinning so much that her cheeks ached. She couldn't believe that she was getting a pony of her own!

As they walked across the yard, a line of horses and ponies poked their heads over their stall doors, looking at Clara curiously as she passed. Clara felt her heart beating faster – one of them could be hers!

"Mr and Mrs Walker?" A lady was hurrying across the yard to meet them, wiping her hands on her jodhpurs. She was tall, and her red hair was tied up in a messy bun with bits of straw sticking out of it. She was wearing a navy jumper with a galloping white horse logo and "Hollyhock Stables" stitched on to it. "I'm Sally Archer, the stable owner."

"I'm George. This is Lizzie – and our

daughter, Clara." Dad introduced them.

Sally looked at Clara. Her brown eyes crinkled as she smiled. "My daughter Milly's about your age." She pointed over to a field where a girl was riding a grey pony around a series of jumps, watched by a stable hand. Wild, curly red hair was sticking out from underneath her helmet. As they watched, the girl leant forward and the pony leapt gracefully over one jump, then the next. Clara felt like clapping. *Maybe one day I'll be able to do that!* she thought to herself.

Clara jumped as Dad put his hand on her shoulder. "Clara is the reason we're here," he explained. "As I said on the phone, we need a pony who's going to be safe for a beginner."

"Absolutely," Sally nodded. "I have the perfect one." She grinned at Clara. "Do you want to meet Honey?"

U